Enid Blyton

Here's

THE
NAUGHTIEST
GIRL

Have you read them all?

Enid Blyton

Here's

THE NAUGHTIEST GIRL

WHYTELEAFE

CHAO · ET · PERTINACIA

Illustrated by Kate Hindley

Hodder
Children's
Books

a division of Hachette Children's Books

Text copyright © Hodder & Stoughton Ltd, 1997
Illustrations copyright © Hodder & Stoughton Ltd, 2014

First published in Great Britain in Enid Blyton's Omnibus
by George Newnes in 1952
This edition published in 2014

The right of Enid Blyton to be identified as the Author of
the Work has been asserted by her in accordance with the
Copyright, Designs and Patents Act 1988

1

A Catalogue record for this book is available from the British Library

ISBN 978 1 444 91885 4

Printed and bound in Great Britain by
Clays Ltd, St Ives plc

The paper and board used in this paperback by Hodder Children's Books
are natural recyclable products made from wood grown in sustainable
forests. The manufacturing processes conform to the environmental
regulations of the country of origin.

Hodder Children's Books
a division of Hachette Children's Books
338 Euston Road, London NW1 3BH
An Hachette UK company

www.hodderchildrens.co.uk

CONTENTS

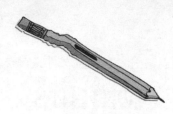

INTRODUCTION

by Cressida Cowell

bestselling author of the
How to Train Your Dragon series

Like so many, many children before and after me, Enid Blyton's books played a crucial role in turning my nine-year-old self into a passionate reader.

That is because Enid Blyton had an extraordinary knack for writing the kind of books that children actually *want* to read, rather than the kind of books that adults think they *should* read.

Enid Blyton could tap into children's dreams, children's desires, children's wishes, with pin-point accuracy. She knew that every child, however good and well-behaved they might look on the outside, secretly longed to be Elizabeth Allen, the naughtiest kid in the school. I'm afraid I entirely cheered Elizabeth on, as she defied her parents, the headmistresses, her schoolmates, and the very serious School Meetings. If anything, I wanted her to be even naughtier.

But the Naughtiest Girl books were really my favourite of Enid Blyton's school stories because of Whyteleafe, a very different school from Malory Towers or St Clare's. What if there could be a school in which discipline was administered by the children rather than the adults? In which all money was given in at the start of the term and distributed amongst the children along socialist lines? Wouldn't this be the kind of school that children would actually *want* to go to, rather than the kind of school that children *have* to go to?

It was an interesting proposition to a nine-year-old, and it remains an interesting proposition.

I hope you enjoy this story as much as I did when *I* was nine years old.

Cressida Cowell

CHAPTER ONE

BACK AT WHYTELEAFE SCHOOL

IT WAS the summer term at Whyteleafe School. All the children were back again – Elizabeth, Julian, Harry, John, Martin, Rosemary and the rest. They rushed round the school excitedly, glad to be back.

'Summer term! My favourite term!' said Elizabeth Allen, pleased. 'Hi, Julian – come and look at my new tennis racket!'

Julian came over, humming a little song. His green eyes twinkled at Elizabeth. 'Hallo,' he said. 'What are you going to be this term, Elizabeth? Naughtiest girl in the school? Best girl? Silliest?'

Elizabeth laughed and gave Julian a punch. 'I'm a monitor, as you jolly well know,' she said. 'I'm going to do my best, and be a monitor all the term – not be chucked out in the middle, as I was last term. What about *you*?'

'Oh, I'm going to do my best, too – but I've got all sorts of bests,' said Julian, grinning. 'I'll beat you at work this term, for one thing – and I'll beat you at

1

tennis – and I'll beat you at thinking out a few little tricks to make life cheerful – and . . .'

'Oh, Julian – I *hope* you'll think of a few tricks,' said Elizabeth. 'But please don't put sneezing powder in the pages of my books again – honestly, it's awful to *have* to keep on and on sneezing without stopping.'

'Right,' said Julian, 'I'll make a note of it!'

Elizabeth was just going to say something more when she caught sight of a boy in the distance. He was so like Julian that she stared in surprise. Same black untidy hair, same green eyes – but what a sulky face!

'Look – there's somebody who looks very like you,' said Elizabeth. 'He must be a new boy.'

Julian turned. 'Yes – that's a cousin of mine. He's got rather a big opinion of himself, as you'll soon find out. He didn't want to come to Whyteleafe School at all.'

'Why ever not?' said Elizabeth, who simply couldn't *imagine* anyone not wanting to come.

'Well – he's not very fond of *me*,' said Julian. 'He doesn't like people who can do things better than he can – and he'll be in our form.'

'And when you use *your* brains you'll be top whenever you want to!' said Elizabeth. 'Even against me!'

'That's easy,' said Julian, and got another punch. 'But, quite seriously, Elizabeth, go slow with Patrick –

he can be very spiteful. Don't play the heavy monitor with him too soon or too much.'

'I shall tick him off if he doesn't toe the line,' said Elizabeth at once. 'How will he behave, do you think?'

'A bit like *you* behaved when you first came!' said Julian, twinkling at her. 'Don't you remember? You were the Naughtiest Girl in the School – and you meant to be, too! The things you did!'

Elizabeth went bright pink. 'You needn't keep reminding me of that first term,' she said. 'I was awful. I just can't think how I could have behaved like that.'

'Well, I wasn't there then,' said Julian, 'but I've heard plenty about it. I bet you'll always be known as the Naughtiest Girl, even if you go on being a monitor for the rest of your school days and end up as Head-Girl!'

'Gosh – I'd never be that,' said Elizabeth. 'Whoever heard of a Naughtiest Girl ending up as Head? Here comes your cousin, Julian.'

Julian swung round. 'Hallo, Patrick,' he said. 'Finding your way about a bit? This is Elizabeth. She's a friend of mine and if you want any help in anything, go to her, because she's a monitor.'

'I'm not likely to go to any friend of yours for help!' said Patrick in a high and mighty voice. 'And, by the way, you don't need to spread around the news that

3

I'm your cousin – I'm not really proud of having you for a cousin! Too swollen-headed for my taste!'

He went off, hands in pockets. Julian glared after him. 'If he wasn't new I'd shake him till his teeth rattled!' he said.

Elizabeth was indignant, too. 'What a cheek from a new boy!' she said. 'Well, he won't cheek *me*! If he does I'll report him.'

A bell rang just then, and everyone hurried in to a meal. Elizabeth scrambled for her place at table. She beamed round at everyone. How good it was to be back among all her friends! John Terry grinned at her across the table.

'Going to help in the garden this term?' he called. 'Have you seen all the seeds that have come up since last term? We shall have a fine show this summer.'

John was partly responsible for the gardens of the school. He loved gardening and was very good at it. Elizabeth nodded back at him. 'Yes – of course I'll help. I love messing about in the garden.'

Elizabeth was going to be busy this term! She meant to ride each day on one of the school ponies. She meant to practise her tennis hard and get into one of the school teams. She meant to help John with the gardens. She was determined to beat Julian as top of the form whenever she could, and that meant a lot of hard work – and she meant to be a good monitor.

Somebody else meant to beat Julian, too! That was Patrick, his cousin. Patrick was jealous of Julian – he had always been glad when he had heard that his cousin didn't work hard at school, and had continually been bottom. He knew that Julian had good brains, and it pleased him that he hadn't used them.

All the same, he hadn't wanted to go to Whyteleafe School. 'Mixed boys and girls!' he thought, scornfully. 'I'd rather go to an all-boys' school. Look at that Elizabeth now – fancy me having to take orders from a girl! Well – I shan't pay much attention to *her*, anyway!'

He set himself to make a good impression on the others in his form. He entered into everything, and because he was good at games, and could be very comical when he tried, he was soon well-liked.

He hadn't Julian's gift of making extraordinary noises – but how he wished he had! Julian could cluck exactly like a hen laying an egg – he could buzz like a blue-bottle fly, drone like a bumble-bee, and make very strange noises like nothing at all.

Patrick had often tried to imitate noises, but he couldn't. For one thing everyone knew he was making them, and that gave the game away.

'Nobody ever knows that Julian is doing the noises,' thought Patrick enviously. 'Last Christmas, when he came to us for a party, he imitated a dog whining, and we all hunted round the house for ages – and though I looked and looked at Julian, I *couldn't* see a single movement of his mouth or throat.'

Patrick soon found that Whyteleafe wasn't at all the 'sissy' kind of school he had expected. His class worked hard and played hard, practically every boy or girl had a hobby, and if anything went wrong it was reported at the big Meeting held by the school each week.

This was a kind of Parliament, at which everything was discussed frankly by the children themselves. Complaints were heard, grumbles were made and set right, money was distributed evenly, plans were made.

Rita and William, the head-boy and head-girl, presided. If punishments had to be meted out, they said what they were to be. Twelve monitors sat on the platform with them – a kind of jury, Elizabeth always thought. She was very proud to be on the platform, sitting alongside the twelve other monitors.

At first Patrick had been pleased to hear that he was to be in Julian's form. He had frequently heard his father and mother say what a pity it was that a boy with good brains like Julian should so often be bottom. He didn't know that the term before Julian had begun to use his brains well, and could always be top of the form if he wanted to be!

So it was a shock to him to find that in the first week's marks Julian was top, Elizabeth was second, and he was tied third with somebody else.

'I thought you made a point of being at the bottom of the form,' he said to Julian. 'Or so I always heard.'

'You heard right,' said Julian, quite amiably. 'I just didn't happen to want to be top, that was all. But I do now. Did *you* want to be top, Patrick? Bad luck that I happen to be using my brains this term, isn't it?'

Patrick turned away. All right – he'd work harder still. He wasn't going to play second fiddle to Julian. He pondered over his tennis. He was good at that. He would take special coaching and practise hard – Julian wasn't much good at tennis! It would do him good to be taken down a peg!

Then one day he came up against Elizabeth. She was the only person in the form he didn't try to be nice to. She was Julian's friend and a monitor – that was enough for Patrick! He hardly ever addressed a word to her, and if ever she came up to a group he was with he walked away.

Elizabeth laughed at first, but soon it infuriated her. She longed to pull him up for something, but the chance didn't come for three weeks.

Then a notice was put on the board for a meeting. 'Meeting of the Garden Committee, at five o'clock sharp,' said the notice. 'All the first form must attend as well, as volunteers are wanted to help with the weeding.'

Patrick was in the first form. He saw the notice and ignored it. Why should he go? He wasn't interested in gardening, he hated weeding, and he certainly wasn't going to volunteer to do anything in the gardens!

He went off to have a quiet practice by himself, taking his racket and tennis balls with him. There was a wall at the side of the school against which he could hit the balls and strike them continually on the rebound.

So, when the meeting gathered, Patrick was not there! John, who was in charge, looked round. 'Are we all here?' he said.

'No. Patrick isn't,' said Elizabeth at once. 'I bet I know where he is, too! Practising hitting balls against the side-wall. I saw him pass the window with his racket.'

'Oh! Well, he's got to come,' said John. 'You are a monitor, Elizabeth. Fetch him, will you?'

'Right,' said Elizabeth, pleased at being able to make Patrick 'toe the line' for once. 'I can hear the thud-thud of the balls against the wall now. I'll bring him along at once!'

And off she went, quite sure she could make Patrick obey her!

CHAPTER TWO

PATRICK COMES UP
AGAINST ELIZABETH

ELIZABETH HURRIED round to the side of the school. Thud, thud, thud, she heard the balls being hit regularly against the wall.

She turned the corner and called out to Patrick. 'Hey! You're supposed to be at the Garden Meeting. You'd better come at once.'

'Get out of my way, please,' said Patrick. 'I'm practising.'

Elizabeth glared. 'John sent me,' she said.

'All right. I send you back,' said Patrick, almost hitting Elizabeth with one of the balls, as he sent it against the wall near her.

'Don't be an idiot,' said Elizabeth, trying not to lose her temper. 'You know I'm a monitor, don't you? Well, you've *got* to come when you're told. It's no good having monitors unless they're obeyed, you know that.'

'I'm not obeying a girl,' said Patrick. 'Do go away.

I shall get annoyed with you in a minute.'

Elizabeth promptly proceeded to get even more annoyed with the infuriating Patrick. She rushed at him and wrenched away his racket. He was so taken by surprise that he let it slip out of his hands.

Then Elizabeth raced away at top speed with it! Patrick tore after her in a rage. Elizabeth turned a corner and deftly threw the racket into a middle of a bush. Then on she went without stopping, back to the Meeting.

She arrived there, panting. Before she could say a word to the startled Meeting, Patrick arrived, too, fuming. 'Where's my racket? How *dare* you snatch it like that? Elizabeth, what have you done with my racket?'

Elizabeth said nothing. John looked surprised, but pointed to a seat. 'Sit down, Patrick,' he said. 'We've been waiting for you?'

'I haven't come to your silly Meeting,' said Patrick, furiously. 'I've come after Elizabeth for my racket!'

'*Sit down*,' ordered John. 'You're at the Meeting now, and here you'll stay. You won't get your racket till the Meeting is over – and not then if you don't behave yourself!'

Patrick was so surprised at John's determined voice that he sat down. He looked all round for his racket, making up his mind to snatch it and go. But he couldn't see it, which was not surprising, as it was still outside in the bushes!

Patrick didn't hear a word of the Meeting. He glared at Elizabeth's triumphant face. He scowled at the little smile on Julian's. Julian was amused at Elizabeth's method of bringing his unwilling cousin to the Meeting, and he wondered where she had put the racket.

Elizabeth forgot about Patrick in her interest in the Meeting, She was very fond of gardening, and John regarded her as one of his right-hand helpers. He kept consulting her, and she was pleased.

She didn't notice that the sky had clouded over and that it had begun to rain. It was only when it suddenly pelted against the window that she looked out and saw the torrents of rain that were falling. Even then she didn't think about the racket outside in the bushes.

She didn't think of it till the Meeting was over. Then John turned to the bored and sulky Patrick. 'Now you can have your racket back from Elizabeth,' he said. 'And please remember if a Meeting of the whole form is arranged, you've got to come to it.'

Patrick scowled. Elizabeth suddenly remembered where she had put his racket – in the middle of the bushes. Goodness – had it got wet in the rain? She knew it was a new racket, and that Patrick was intensely proud of it.

PATRICK COMES UP AGAINST ELIZABETH

She wished she could go and get it out of the bushes and dry it before she gave it to Patrick. But he gave her no chance to do that. He followed close at her heels when she went out of the room. She walked out of the garden door and went to the wet bushes. It was still pouring with rain. She fished out the soaked racket.

Patrick stared at it in horror and anger. 'You beast! You flung my new racket there in the pouring rain! It'll be ruined.'

'It wasn't raining when I put it there, you know it wasn't,' said Elizabeth.

'Well, why didn't you go out and get it when the rain began?' said Patrick furiously. 'You left it there on purpose! You *meant* the rain to spoil it! Just like a girl!'

'I *didn't* mean to spoil it!' said Elizabeth angrily. 'I didn't even notice it was raining till nearly the end of the Meeting – and then I forgot all about your racket. It's your fault for not coming to the Meeting, so that I had to fetch you!'

Patrick was wiping the strings with his handkerchief. He was trembling with rage and disappointment. His lovely new racket!

'I hate you for this,' he said. 'Now you'll go and laugh about it with Julian, and be glad you've ruined my racket – there wasn't a better one in the school! You'll both be glad it's spoilt!'

'Patrick, don't be silly,' said Elizabeth. 'Look – I'm very sorry I didn't think of your racket being out in the rain. If I'd remembered it, I'd have gone to get it at once. And of *course* Julian and I won't be glad if it's spoilt.'

'Yes, you will. I detest you both,' said Patrick, his face bright red, and his green eyes flaming like Julian's did when he was angry. 'I'll get even with you! You're just exactly the kind of mean, catty girl I'd expect my cocky cousin to be friends with!'

He tucked his racket under his arm, and walked off in a rage, the rain still pouring down as he went. Elizabeth shook back her wet curls. Blow! What an idiot she had been to forget the racket when it began to rain. She really was sorry about that.

Julian met her as she went back. 'Gosh, you *are* wet!' he said. 'What happened? Where did you put his racket? *Not* out in the rain, I hope!'

'Yes, I did – but I didn't mean to,' said Elizabeth, soberly, and she told Julian what had happened, and what Patrick had said. 'He never liked me before, Julian, and now he's really furious with me. He hates you, too, doesn't he? Oh, dear, I do hope he won't do anything silly now. He really looked as if he'd like to hit me with his racket!'

'He probably would have if he hadn't thought his

racket would be hurt more than you would!' said Julian. 'Cheer up – what can he do to pay you back – or me either? Nothing that matters. Come on into the gym – there'll be games going on there.'

Patrick made a great fuss about his precious racket. He told everyone what had happened. He spoke of having to get all the strings replaced, and when the next School Meeting was held, he actually got up and asked for the money to have his racket completely restrung!

He stood up when William said, 'Any complaints, please?' Anyone could then stand up and lodge a complaint, big or small. Patrick leapt to his feet before anyone else.

'I have a complaint!' he said. 'Against a monitor, Elizabeth Allen. She left my racket out in the rain and it's ruined. I want to ask for money out of the school money-box so that I can pay for it to be restrung.'

'Elizabeth – perhaps you'd like to say something about this,' said William, the head-boy, in surprise.

Elizabeth stood up, feeling embarrassed. She related truthfully what had happened, and added that she was very sorry about the racket being left out in the wet. 'But it wasn't for very long,' she said, 'and I'm sure, William, that it doesn't need restringing.'

'Have you the racket with you?' William asked Patrick. 'No? Well, go and get it. I know a good bit

15

about rackets and I can tell you at once what wants doing.'

Patrick went to get the racket with a very bad grace. He came back and gave it to William. 'Look – there's a string gone already!' he said, pointing to the broken string. Elizabeth stared in dismay.

William examined the racket very carefully. Then he put it down and looked sternly at Patrick. 'That string is not frayed or split,' he said. 'It has been cut. The racket does not need restringing – only that one string needs putting in. Who cut it, Patrick? Tell me that?'

'How should I know?' said Patrick, sulkily.

There was a short silence. 'Now listen,' said William, 'you yourself must pay for that one string being renewed. The rain had nothing to do with its being broken. I think you know that very well. Every other string is perfectly all right. If you still want the whole racket restrung, you can save up the two pounds you are allowed each week, and pay for it yourself – but it will take you more than a term's money!'

Patrick snatched up his racket without a word. He glanced at Elizabeth. She looked scornfully back. So he had actually cut a string in his own racket to try and make out that she had really spoilt it by leaving it for a few minutes in the rain! What a thing to do!

PATRICK COMES UP AGAINST ELIZABETH

Patrick made a sudden face at her, and then left the platform with his racket. He passed by Julian and saw a little smile on his face. He almost hit him with the racket! 'I'll pay you both back!' he said in a whisper, and marched right out of the hall.

'Don't call him back,' said Rita, the head-girl, to William. 'He's a new boy. He's got to learn our ways! Now – any more complaints?'

There were none. Nor were there any grumbles. William hammered his fist on the table as a little talking broke out.

'You may dismiss,' he said. 'The Meeting is over.'

Elizabeth sped to Julian. 'Oh, Julian – isn't Patrick MEAN! Did he really cut that string, do you think? It did look exactly as if it had been cut.'

'Of course he did,' said Julian. 'He's an idiot. We'd better look out for him now, Elizabeth. He may really try to pay you back!'

'Pooh! *I'm* not afraid of Patrick,' said Elizabeth. And she wasn't!

CHAPTER THREE

JULIAN'S LITTLE TRICK

PATRICK BROODED over the whole affair. He had a sulky nature; and could not easily forget anything that upset him. He completely ignored Julian and Elizabeth, turning his back on them whenever they came near.

This only amused them, however, and in the end Julian turned the joke against Patrick by calling out warningly whenever he or Elizabeth went near him:

'Be ready to turn your back, Patrick. Here we come again! Hurry up and turn, or you'll see us!'

Patrick tried in vain to think of some big, triumphant way of getting back at Julian and Elizabeth. He was bitterly disappointed that Julian was so good at his class work. His cousin had always been so don't-carish over that, so he had heard, and Patrick had looked forward to crowing over him and being top each week.

But no matter how hard Patrick worked, Julian seemed to be able to work harder! Julian had brilliant brains, found learning easy, and was determined that Patrick should not once beat him in marks.

Patrick was second one week – beating Elizabeth. But Julian was still triumphantly top, a full ten marks ahead of Patrick. Miss Ranger, the class mistress, was amazed at the high marks that Julian, Patrick and Elizabeth showed each week! She didn't know how hard they were vying with one another.

Patrick decided to concentrate on tennis, and beat Julian at that. Julian was good, but he wasn't keen on being in any of the school tennis teams. He said it meant too much hard work to keep in practice!

'All the same, Julian, you'd *better* get some practice in,' said Elizabeth, 'because that cousin of yours is getting jolly good. I watched him playing with some boys older than he is, and he was as good as they were. He'll be in one of the top teams if you don't look out – and won't he crow over you! Do, do beat him, Julian.'

'Blow you, Elizabeth,' said Julian, and pretended to sigh heavily. 'What with working like a slave to keep ahead of you and Patrick in class – and now having to tire myself out with tennis, to beat Patrick, my life's not worth living! What about *you* taking him on at tennis?'

'I do try – but he's got a much harder serve than I have,' said Elizabeth, honestly. 'Go on, Julian – you can be *much* better than Patrick, and I'd jump for joy

19

if you got into the second team, which is what *he* wants to do!'

Julian tried – and Patrick had the disappointment of being well and truly beaten by his cousin when they played against each other two weeks after that! Patrick hadn't realized that Julian had become so good, and he was humiliated and disappointed.

'If he gets into the second team instead of me I'll hit him on the head!' thought Patrick, going off the court with a very gloomy face. 'He doesn't really care about tennis, and I do. He's only doing it to spite me.'

'Jolly good, Julian!' said Elizabeth, giving him a thump on the back as he came whistling off the court, having collected all the balls that Patrick had been too annoyed to pick up. 'Did you see his face? He looked as sick as a hen left out in the rain!'

'Oh well – it's rather a shame really,' said Julian. 'I don't care if I'm good at tennis or not, and he does. But seeing that he only wants to have the pleasure of crowing over me if he beats me, I don't mind beating *him!*'

'Yes – and you *don't* crow!' said Elizabeth. 'I hope you get into the second team and go and play against Hickling Green School, Julian – that's always such a good outing.'

Julian began to get a bit bored with his extra efforts

at lessons and tennis. He was also working very hard at making a model aeroplane, for he was very clever with his hands. All this concentration made him feel suddenly stale.

He began to plan a little pleasure for his form. Strange noises? Something weird up the chimney? He thought hard, and a sudden grin came on his face.

'The chimney! I sit fairly near the fireplace, and I could work something in the chimney. Now – let's see.'

When his classroom was empty, Julian went in cautiously. He crouched down by the chimney and looked up it. It was rather narrow. A broad mantelpiece was over the fireplace, and this Julian examined very carefully. He had noticed last winter that, when the wind was in a certain direction, little eddies of smoke came out from under the mantelpiece. He was looking for the crack from which they must have come.

'There must be a crack or a hole somewhere,' thought Julian, 'or the smoke wouldn't get out from the chimney under the mantelpiece and into the room. Ah – here it is!'

He had found the crack, where the cement had worn away. He took a chisel and made the hole considerably bigger. He poked the chisel some way through, and then decided that the hole was big enough for his purpose.

He took a piece of string and tied a penknife to one end. He poked the knife through the hole, and gave it a push. It clattered into the chimney, fell down and suddenly appeared in the hearth!

'Ha! Good!' said Julian, pleased. He still had hold of the string that went into the hole. He knocked a small tack in on the underside of the wooden mantelpiece and then tied the string to it firmly. He tested it. Yes, it held well.

He undid the knife from the other end of the string, which hung down the chimney into the fireplace. He then disappeared into the corridor and fetched a small bell that was kept there to summon Matron if she was needed in a hurry.

He went back into the classroom and carefully tied the bell to the end of the string that hung down the chimney. Then he undid the other end from the nail, and pulled it, so that the bell was dragged out of sight up the chimney!

Then Julian gave a little tug to the string he held, and a muffled and rather weird tinkle came from up the chimney!

Julian chuckled. He ran the end of the string under the mantelpiece and held it in place by little staples he drove into the wood. The string fell down the side of the fireplace just by his chair. Julian sat down and bent over his desk, holding the end of the string in his hand. He tugged it – and a mournful little jingle came from the inside of the chimney!

'A nice little treat for the class this afternoon,' thought Julian, and tied the string to one leg of his chair.

Miss Ranger took the class that afternoon. It was a geography lesson, rather dull. Julian waited for a moment of silence and then gave the string tied to his chair leg a little tug.

At once it pulled the bell hanging in the chimney and a sudden little jingle sounded in the room. Everyone looked up. Julian did too. He meant to be as surprised as anyone else!

He tugged the string again. Jingle-tinkle-tink went the bell, obligingly.

'What's that noise?' asked Miss Ranger, puzzled. 'It sounds exactly like a bell somewhere. Where is it ringing? Has anyone got a bell with them this afternoon?'

'No, Miss Ranger!' chorused everyone except Julian. He tugged again, and the bell jangled quite loudly.

'Well – it *sounds* up the chimney!' said John. 'But how could a bell ring in the chimney?'

'It couldn't,' said Miss Ranger, firmly. 'So we won't ask you or anyone else to go crawling up the chimney to look for bells there, John. Stand up, everyone, and put your hands above your heads. If anyone has a bell, and can ring it when his hands are above his head, he will be clever!'

Everyone stood with hands above their heads, Julian too. Jingle-jingle-jing! The bell rang again. Julian had managed to get his foot to the string and jerk it! A babble of noise broke out at once.

'Nobody's got a bell and yet it rang again! Miss Ranger, what is it? Miss Ranger, it's peculiar! Where is it, do you suppose? Can't we look for it?'

'No,' said Miss Ranger, firmly, imagining a bevy of excited children crawling over the room and completely ruining the rest of the geography lesson. 'Bell or no bell, we go on with the lesson. Sit!'

They sat and the bell immediately rang a merry peal. 'Take no notice,' commanded Miss Ranger, who was just as puzzled as anyone else, but determined not to show it. 'I have only one more thing to say about this bell – and that is, if I find out that anyone in this class is plaguing us with a jingling bell, I shall do a bit of plaguing myself – and the culprit will be very, very sorry for himself!'

After that they all settled down, and although the bell rang plaintively at intervals, and the children began to giggle each time, nobody dared to take much notice of it.

As soon as the class was ended and Miss Ranger was safely out of the room, John ran to the chimney. 'It sounded as if it came from here,' he said. 'I know it did!'

He put his hand up the chimney and groped about. Tinkle, jing! He had touched the bell!

'It *is* up here!' he cried. 'I thought so. But how on earth did it get there?' He turned and saw Julian's grinning face. He laughed. 'Julian! It's one of your ridiculous tricks – but HOW did you get the bell hanging there?'

'Easy!' said Julian, and showed the interested class how he had managed it. Only one of them sneered. That was Patrick, of course.

'What a childish trick! I'm sure Miss Ranger will be very scornful about it when I tell her.'

He was immediately pushed down hard on a chair and three or four children pinned him down firmly. 'Sneak! Tell-tale! We'll never speak to you again if you do that.'

'All right, all right. I was only joking,' said Patrick, trying to push them off, afraid of making them dislike him. They let him go.

John had pulled the bell down from the chimney and now it lay on the floor nearby. Patrick gave it a vicious kick, and it slid jangling over the floor. Julian smiled broadly. 'Taking it out on the bell instead of on me, I suppose?' he said. 'Pity you can't see a joke, Patrick.'

The next day a really peculiar thing happened. It was Miss Ranger's class again, this time in maths. All the children were copying sums down from the blackboard, when once more there was a curious noise from the chimney.

Everyone raised their heads and grinned. Was this another trick of old Julian's? But he looked as surprised as they did.

The noise came again, a struggling kind of noise, then came a series of high squeaks, and a little soot fell down the chimney.

'Now whatever is *this*?' said Miss Ranger, exasperated. She suddenly thought of Julian and his tricks. She looked straight at him. 'Julian – is this one of your tricks? Answer me truthfully, please.'

'No, Miss Ranger. It isn't one of my tricks. I can't *imagine* what is going on in the chimney,' said Julian, quite truthfully.

Squeak, squeak, chirri-chirri-chirrup!

Patrick got up. 'Julian's not telling the truth!' he said. 'It was *his* chimney trick yesterday – and it's his trick again today! Look up the chimney and you'll see his trick, Miss Ranger! He's a frightful fibber!'

CHAPTER FOUR

PATRICK IN TROUBLE

THE WHOLE class stared at Patrick in amazement and disgust. Julian shrugged his shoulders. 'I do assure you, Miss Ranger, I haven't the faintest idea what is going on up our chimney,' he said.

'You DO know! You've put something up there again!' cried Patrick, in a fury. 'Just to suck up to the class and make them think you're marvellous!'

'That's enough,' said Miss Ranger. And then, quite suddenly, with another series of squeaks and chirps, something fell down the chimney and came to rest with a little thud on the hearth!

'Chirrup!' it said, feebly. The children stared at it. 'A baby starling – and golly, here comes another!' cried Harry, as a second black little creature arrived beside the other. 'There must have been a starling's nest up the chimney – and these two have wriggled out and fallen down. Poor little things!'

'Sucks to you, Patrick,' said Elizabeth, in delight. 'You can't say that Julian built the starling's nest or turned out the young starlings, can you! Sucks to you!'

'Elizabeth, I don't like that vulgar expression,' said Miss Ranger, coldly. 'John, take those two poor little creatures and put them outside in a bush where perhaps their starling parents may see them and feed them. Patrick, take that scowl off your face.'

'It was Julian who put the bell up the chimney yesterday, anyhow!' blurted out Patrick. 'So what are you going to do about *that*?'

'Nothing,' said Miss Ranger, calmly. 'Sit down in your places, everyone. We are now going on with our lesson – and I must warn you all that I do NOT feel in the mood for any more disturbances, whispers or giggles.'

The children bent over their books, but there were many scornful glances thrown at Patrick. He bent over his book too, kicking himself for thinking that was a trick of Julian's – and for being unable to prevent himself from blurting out about the bell-trick.

He hurried out in front of the others afterwards, afraid that they would take him to task. He ran to get his racket, meaning to go and bang the balls at the side-wall, to work off some of his anger.

But the class followed him, and soon he was surrounded by an angry little company. Elizabeth advanced on him, her eyes gleaming. 'I may as well tell you,' she began, 'that sooner or later complaints will be made about you at the next School Meeting, and—'

'Shut up,' said Patrick, and threw a ball up into the air to hit against the wall. 'Go away, all of you. I'm fed up with this school – and most of all I'm fed up with my grinning, very-very-clever cousin – and with Elizabeth, the cocky, high-and-mighty monitor!'

Elizabeth tried to grab his racket, to make him stop playing about – he should be *made* to listen to what was being said! But Patrick swung it away and then raised it again to hit another ball.

He hit Elizabeth instead! Crack! The racket descended heavily on her right shoulder and she yelled. Julian leapt at Patrick, his face blazing. Coward! To hit a girl!

He caught Patrick by the shoulder, and held him tightly. 'We'll call a Meeting tonight!' he said. 'We'll say that for the rest of this term Patrick shall not play tennis again! We'll confiscate his racket for hitting Elizabeth.'

'Let me go! said Patrick, fiercely. 'It was an accident – but I'm glad I hit her, all the same. She deserved it! Call your Meeting if you like – I shan't be there! And I'll tell you this, Julian – you're only doing this to keep me out of the second team, because you want to be in it yourself, instead of me!'

He flung Julian off, made a dive under the arms held up to stop him, and tore away at top speed.

'Let him go,' said Rosemary. 'Elizabeth, are you hurt?'

'No. Not really,' said Elizabeth. 'Only bruised. Isn't he a beast, though? Julian, it's bad luck on you to have a cousin like that!'

'We'll send him to Coventry! We won't speak to him for the rest of the term! We'll see that he doesn't touch a racket again!' said several voices.

'Telling a fib about Julian!'

'Wasn't it strange, though, those birds falling down the chimney the very day after Julian had put a bell up there!'

'Jolly decent of Miss Ranger not to say anything more about it when Patrick blurted out the truth,' said John.

A monitor from the second form appeared round the corner. 'I say! What's happening? Didn't you hear the bell, you idiots? You won't get anything to eat if you don't hurry up. I've been sent to find you.'

'Oh goodness – we never even *heard* the bell!' said Elizabeth, still rubbing her shoulder. 'Come on, everyone. All this has made me feel jolly hungry.'

Patrick did not come in to the meal. Miss Ranger did not inquire about him. She knew that he was upset and probably did not want to appear in public just then. Nobody bothered about him. Let him miss his meal if he wanted to. Do him good! That was what most of his class thought.

Elizabeth and Julian did not attempt to call a big School Meeting that night after all. When they had cooled down a bit it seemed rather silly to air the grievances of the first form in front of the whole school.

'After all, the next Meeting is on Saturday,' said Elizabeth. 'If Patrick doesn't behave himself for the rest of the week, we'll make a formal complaint about him then, and deal with him. I don't really believe he *meant* to hit me, Julian.'

'Well, perhaps not,' said Julian. 'He's an unpleasant bit of work, though, isn't he? I wish he hadn't come here. It's hard enough to beat *you* in order to be top of the form – it's getting to be even harder to beat Patrick – and I'm really a bit tired of practising my tennis at every moment, just so that he won't be in the second team!'

'It's jolly good for you to work hard at things!' said Elizabeth, remembering how don't-carish Julian had been the term before. 'I wonder where Patrick is? He hasn't shown up at all.'

'Good thing too,' said Julian. 'I expect he doesn't want to face the form. They'll do to him what he's been doing to you and me – they'll turn their backs whenever he appears!'

'Where did you put his racket?' asked Elizabeth. 'Have you hidden it so that he can't get it?'

'Yes. I've put a note in his desk to say that he can have it back if he apologizes to you,' said Julian. 'Otherwise, he won't have it.'

'Oh, dear – I don't really like all this upset,' said Elizabeth. 'It makes me have feelings that aren't at all suitable to a monitor. Even if Patrick comes and apologizes – and I believe he'd rather lose his racket than do that – I shan't feel like accepting his apology. I might say something rude and begin the upset all over again.'

'Well, do,' said Julian with a grin. 'I've no objection!'

'Come and have a game of tennis,' said Elizabeth. 'Let's slash out at the balls and work some of our crossness out of us. Come on!'

So out they went and were soon hitting the balls with a will. When they had finished they looked about for Patrick. Would he come and apologize? He must have seen the note in his desk by now.

But he was still nowhere to be seen!

CHAPTER FIVE

AT MIDNIGHT

THE CHILDREN were allowed to take their tea into the garden that day and have little picnics in friendly groups. That was always fun. Elizabeth, Julian, John, Harry, Rosemary and Joan found a place in the shade by some bushes.

'Anyone seen Patrick?' asked Elizabeth, biting into bread and honey.

'Yes. I saw him coming out of our classroom,' said John. 'I don't know where he is now though. Having tea by himself somewhere, I expect, brooding over his woes.'

'Oh, well – don't let's think about him any more,' said Elizabeth. 'He's keeping out of our way and I'm not surprised.'

They thought no more about Patrick. Elizabeth went back with the others to fetch her prep and do it out-of-doors that lovely warm evening. But it was difficult to learn French verbs when the swallows swooped and darted in the sky, and bees hummed happily in the flowers around. French verbs didn't go well with swallows and bees.

When they all went up to bed Elizabeth looked round once more for Patrick. She hated to go to bed without making up a quarrel, though she had often done so.

She called to Julian as he went to the boys' dormitory. 'Julian! See if Patrick is in your dormy.'

He wasn't. Julian began to feel a bit worried. Where was the idiot? Sulking somewhere? He debated whether or not to report that Patrick hadn't come up to bed. He decided that he wouldn't – not for a little while, anyhow.

'If I do report him, and he's hiding somewhere, waiting till we're all in bed because he's afraid of being jeered at, he'll get into more trouble,' thought Julian. 'And he'll think I've reported him just for that reason – to get him into a row. Blow him! Well, I'll get into bed, and wait till he comes before I go to sleep.'

He told this to John and Harry, who shared the dormy with him and Patrick. They agreed to do the same as Julian – wait till Patrick came before they went to sleep. 'And we won't rag him at all,' said Harry. 'He's had a pretty poor day.'

But – alas for their good resolves – every boy was

fast asleep before five minutes had gone! The girls fell asleep, too – but Elizabeth kept waking up and wondering about Patrick.

As she turned over for about the twelfth time, she thought she heard a rustling of paper. She sat up in bed and groped for what she had heard. Yes – there *was* a bit of paper somewhere in her bed. It must have slipped down there when she had got in. She pulled it out.

She put on her light and read what was written there. It was a note from Patrick!

'ELIZABETH,

You can believe me or not, but I didn't *mean* to hit you, and I apologize for my racket slipping down on your shoulder like that. It was partly your fault for grabbing at it. I wish I hadn't blurted out about Julian's trick, too, but I said it without thinking.

You won't be bothered with me any more. I'm fed up with Whyteleafe and I'm going away tonight as soon as it's dark. I'm going home. It was mean to take my racket away from me. I would have liked to take it with me. There's no use in staying at Whyteleafe – Julian is determined to out-do me in everything – but the tennis isn't fair, because I really *could* do well at that, and I might have got into the

second team.

Nobody likes me now. I don't like anybody either, least of all you. I hope there's a good old upset about me running away – it will serve this beastly school right!

PATRICK'

Elizabeth read this in the greatest horror. She sat staring at the letter in a panic. Patrick must have slid it under the sheet for her to find it when she got into bed, and it had slipped down when she got in. What a pity she hadn't read it hours before – she might have stopped Patrick from being such an idiot as to run away!

She slipped on her dressing-gown and went to Julian's dormy. She put her head round the door and called softly: 'Julian! Julian!'

Julian was a light sleeper. He awoke at once. He went to the door. 'What are you doing here?' he said. 'You'll get into a frightful row.'

'It's about Patrick,' said Elizabeth. 'Come down into our classroom and read a note he's left in my bed. It's urgent, Julian.'

Julian put on his dressing-gown and the two went down into their classroom. They did not dare to switch on the light, but shone their torches on to the note. Julian read it in dismay.

'I say! The fathead! We'll have the police looking for him, and Whyteleafe in the papers, and there'll be a frightful disturbance,' he groaned. 'What in the world are we to do?'

'When do you suppose he went?' whispered Elizabeth. 'He wouldn't go till it was dark, would he? It can't have been dark very long because these summer nights are light for ages. Should we snoop round a bit and see if we can see anything of him?'

'We could. But he'll be gone,' said Julian, feeling most uncomfortable at the thought of having to go and wake the head-master and two head-mistresses, and show them the note. He began to feel that he hadn't come very well out of the affair himself. It was possible that the grown-ups might think him rather mean to have deliberately tried to out-shine Patrick, and not give him a chance to make good at anything.

There was no sign of Patrick, so the two decided most reluctantly to go and tell someone in authority. They made their way down the back stairs of the school, meaning to go through to the hall and up the stairs to where the staff bedrooms were.

And then, as they went down the back stairs, they heard a sound. They stopped. What was that? Where did it come from?

'It's in the cupboard,' whispered Julian. 'Look – over

40

there, where all the sports things are kept. But Patrick can't be there!'

Another sound came from the cupboard – a sound as if the door was being jiggled a little. The two crept up to it. The key was in the lock. Julian did not touch the key, but cautiously turned the handle. The door would not open. It was obviously locked on the outside.

'Whoever's in there is locked in,' whispered Julian. They looked at one another. 'It can't be Patrick. He wouldn't go to this cupboard – it's only got spare sports things in.'

Julian spoke quietly at the crack of the door. 'Who's in here?'

A voice answered at once. 'Who's that? I'm locked in here. I'm Patrick. Let me out.'

Elizabeth clutched at Julian joyfully. So Patrick hadn't gone! Julian was glad, too. He put his mouth to the crack again.

'Patrick. It's me, Julian – and Elizabeth's here, too. We found your note just now. You're an idiot. We are idiots, too, so we're quits.'

There was a silence. 'You let me out at once,' came Patrick's voice, rather shaky.

'All right – on one condition,' said Julian. 'Do you promise to give up your mad idea of running off tonight, and will you go straight to bed?'

'No,' said Patrick.

'All right. We're off to bed,' said Julian.

A frantic voice came from inside the cupboard. 'Don't go! It's horrible in here – smelly and lonely and uncomfortable. Let me out. I won't run off. I promise.'

'How did you get locked in here?' asked Julian, still not turning the key.

'Well – I badly wanted to take my racket with me,' said Patrick's voice, 'and I didn't know where it had been hidden. So I looked everywhere. The last place I thought of was this old sports cupboard – but while I was looking someone came along, slammed the door and locked me in.'

'Matron, I expect,' said Julian. 'She's always slamming doors and locking them. Well – I'll let you out.'

He unlocked the door and shone his torch into the cupboard. Patrick was there, blinking, looking very tousled and untidy, and rather white in the face.

Elizabeth felt sorry for him. She slid her arm through his. 'Patrick! I know you didn't mean to hit me! Of *course* I know it. I think we all got silly and excited. We none of us behaved very well.'

'You didn't come to any meals,' said Julian, remembering. 'Aren't you hungry?'

'Yes,' said Patrick going upstairs with them.

'Come and have some of my tuck, then,' said Julian.

'But don't give me away, because we're not supposed to have food at night. Elizabeth, look the other way. Being a monitor, you can't approve!'

'Oh, dear – can't I? But I *do*,' said Elizabeth. 'Patrick, I'll give you back your racket.'

She disappeared. The boys looked at one another. Julian shoved some more biscuits at Patrick. 'I don't *really* want to be in the second team,' said Julian, in a casual, ordinary voice. 'I just thought I would be to show you I *could* be. But all this practising bores me. In any case, you'll always be better than me in that. So go ahead.'

'Oh! Well, thanks,' said Patrick, seeing that this was Julian's way of patching up a quarrel. 'And *I* don't particularly want to slave to be top of the form. You're welcome to that position. We'll – er – split our brains, shall we?'

'Not a bad idea,' said Julian, munching a biscuit himself. 'Easier for us both. Hallo, here's Elizabeth back again.'

Elizabeth came in with the racket.

'Here you are, Patrick – and don't you dare hit me again with it!'

Patrick eagerly took his precious racket. Elizabeth suddenly realized what a tremendous lot he thought of it. She stared at him and he stared back. Then he suddenly smiled.

'Whatever would people think if they saw us all here, munching biscuits at this time of night!' he said. 'Now, don't you go reporting us at the next Meeting, Elizabeth!'

'Come on – we *must* go to bed!' said Julian hearing the clock strike midnight. 'We shall all be bottom of the form if we go on like this – staying up till past midnight!'

They crept upstairs very quietly and said goodnight on the landing. Elizabeth got into bed feeling at peace. Who would have thought things would turn out like this after all? Perhaps Patrick would settle down and be as proud of Whyteleafe as they all were.

Julian got into bed and was asleep at once. Patrick was in bed, too – but he was rather uncomfortable: he had taken his racket with him, feeling that he really couldn't let it out of his sight now; and it was a very hard and knobbly bed-fellow!

'Whyteleafe School's not so bad,' thought Patrick. 'Julian's not so bad, either. And as for Elizabeth, why, she's really quite nice. I'm very much afraid – *very* much afraid – I'm going to like her!'

BONUS BLYTON

Enid Blyton has been one of the world's best-loved storytellers for over 70 years. Her interest in writing began as a child, and before she loved receiving letters from the children who read her books, she enjoyed working with them as a teacher. The Naughtiest Girl stories are inspired by real schools and experiences. Turn the page to learn more about Enid as a child and as a teacher. Afterwards, you might like to write about your school and teachers and the people in *your* class!

THE LIFE AND TIMES OF ENID BLYTON

11 August 1897	Enid Blyton was born in East Dulwich, London. Two brothers are born after her – Hanly (b. 1899) and Carey (b. 1902)
1911	Enid enters a children's poetry competition and is praised for her writing. She's on the path to becoming a bestselling author . . .
1916	Enid begins to train as a teacher in Ipswich. By the time she is 21, she is a fully-qualified Froebel teacher, and starts work at a school in Kent.
1917	Enid's first 'grown-up' publication – three poems in *Nash's Magazine*.
June 1922	Enid's first book is published. It's called *Child Whispers*.
1926	Enid begins editing – and writes – the phenomenal *Sunny Stories for Little Folks* magazine. (She continues in this role for 26 years!)

1927	So vast is Enid's output that she has to learn to type. (But she still writes to children by hand.)
1931	Having married Hugh Pollock in 1924, the couple's first child, Gillian, is born. Imogen, their second daughter, was born in 1935.
1942	The Famous Five is launched with *Five on a Treasure Island*.
1949	The first appearance of *The Secret Seven* and of *Noddy* mark this year as special.
1953	Enid moves away from *Sunny Stories* to launch *Enid Blyton's Magazine*. She is now renowned throughout the world – she even established her own company, called Darrell Waters Limited (the surname of her second husband).
1962	Enid Blyton becomes one of the first and most important children's authors to be published in paperback. Now, she reaches even more readers than ever before.
28 November 1968	Enid dies in her sleep, in a nursing home in Hampstead.

WHAT THEY DID AT
MISS BROWN'S SCHOOL

In 1920, Enid Blyton became a governess to the four
Thompson children, whose ages ranged from four to
ten. The family lived in Surbiton, in Surrey, in a house
called 'Southernhay'. Enid had a small room which
overlooked the garden, and it was there that she wrote
many of her stories. Enid's tiny class often had lessons
outdoors in the summer months.

Enid was very popular with her students, because her
lessons were both practical and creative. She worked
with them to put on performances for which they made
props, costumes and invitations – and even sold tickets.

In 1941, she published a long story called 'What
They Did at Miss Brown's School', which was divided
into monthly episodes. It's been hard to find for many
years, but you can read extracts in these new editions
of the Naughtiest Girl books. The character of Miss
Brown and her tiny class is very much based on Enid
Blyton and her school at the Thompsons' . . .

Here's the next episode . . .

WHAT THEY DID AT
MISS BROWN'S SCHOOL

April. Planning the School Garden.

THE CHILDREN loved the soft warm days of April when the sun shone from a brilliant sky, and great clouds like bunches of cotton-wool swept overhead. Sometimes the rain poured down as the sun shone and then a rainbow arched itself among the clouds, and the children watched it in delight till it slowly faded.

They had been saving up for seed-buying, and one morning Miss Brown asked then to bring their money and to see how much they had. Miss Brown said she would buy the vegetable seeds herself – that should be her share.

'Oh, are we going to grow vegetables too?' asked Susan, in delight. 'As well as planting the beans and peas we grew in our germinators?'

'Oh yes,' said Miss Brown. 'We must have some lettuces and some radishes, and we will plant some mustard and cress again too – plenty of it, so that we can have it for tea three or four times.'

Well, that afternoon the four children went shopping with their teacher. They were excited, because they had been looking out for seed packets and they had seen such a lot in the shops, all so gay and bright, with pictures of flowers on the front.

'Now we must NOT buy cheap seeds,' said Miss Brown. 'That is quite certain. It always pays, in gardening, to buy the best we can afford, because then we shall get finer flowers and better vegetables.'

So they asked the man at the shop which were his *best* seeds, and he showed them the packets. There were so many, of all sorts and kinds, that the children simply didn't know which to choose. So Miss Brown had to help them.

'No, don't have wallflowers,' she said. 'They would not flower till next year. No, Susan, it's no use looking longingly at sweet-williams – they wouldn't flower till next year, either. You want *Annuals*. Look for Annuals – seeds that will flower this same year – not Biennials, which will only flower the second year.'

So then the children examined the packets carefully and looked for the word Annuals. The shopman helped them.

'You can have Shirley poppies, and pretty things they are,' he said. 'Or here is candytuft, as sweet as its name. And there's marigold that will grow anywhere, and nasturtium which isn't particular either. And clarkia that Miss Brown will love for cutting. And you should really have this virginian stock to edge your little garden – it grows as thick as grass, and is as pretty as a picture!'

'Oh, Mr Millet, we don't know *which* to have!' said the children. 'Which shall we choose, Miss Brown?'

'Whichever you like!' laughed Miss Brown. 'Hurry up and choose – I'm going to buy my radish seed.'

'No, see here,' said Mr Millet the shopman, in a low voice, as Miss Brown went to another counter. 'I happen to know that Miss Brown likes a sweet smell – so what about a little mignonette? She'll love a bit of that in the classroom when it's out. And she's very fond of cornflowers too.'

'Well, we'll have both those, then,' said Mary at once, for she was fond of Miss Brown and wanted to please her. 'Look, Mr Millet – here is all the money we have. How many packets will it buy?'

Mr Millet counted it. 'Oh, quite a lot of packets,' he said. 'You choose which you'd like and I'll see if your money will buy them all.'

So this is what they chose – virginian stock, marigolds, nasturtiums that climbed, cornflowers, Shirley poppies, clarkia, mignonette and candytuft.

'Yes, you can have all those,' said Mr Millet, counting the packets. 'And one more, too. Look, here is love-in-a-mist, a pretty blue flower that grows in a mist of fine green leaves – or what about giant sunflowers? They grow taller than I am, and will give you seeds for the birds in the winter.'

'Oh, giant sunflowers, please!' said the children at once. So the nine packets were wrapped up, and then Miss Brown had to hear all about them. She showed them her packets – one of mustard, one of cress, one of radishes and one of lettuce. 'What fun we are going to have!' they all said, as they went out of the shop.

'We will have a look at the garden this afternoon,' said Miss Brown, 'and decide what we must do before we plant our seeds.'

So they had a look at it. Miss Brown had dug it over in the autumn, but it now looked untidy and full of weeds.

'It wants well raking and weeding,' said Miss Brown. 'Who will come after tea and help?'

'I will!' shouted everybody. And everybody came. They took out every weed, and then John raked the whole bed with Miss Brown's big rake. Soon it was smooth and soft, ready for the seeds. The frost had got into the earth and had broken it into powder. Now it was fine and dry in the April sun.

'We will wait for a shower and then plant our seeds when the ground is moist,' said Miss Brown.

The very next morning there was a sharp shower. Mary looked out into the garden. 'Miss Brown!' she cried: 'The garden looks just right for planting!'

'I believe it is!' said Miss Brown. 'Come along out and bring your seeds.'

They all trooped out joyfully. Miss Brown stopped and looked at the seed packets. 'Please sort these packets out into low-growing plants and taller ones,' she said to John. 'It is no use our putting giant sunflowers at the front and the tiny virginian stock at the back!'

It wasn't long before the children decided that the virginian stock must come right at the front for an edging. The mignonette and candytuft could come just behind, for they did not grow very tall. The marigolds could go in that row too. Then must come the cornflowers, the Shirley poppies and the clarkia. At the back would be the nasturtiums climbing up Miss Brown's trellis, and also the big sunflowers.

'That should make a lovely bed,' said Miss Brown. 'Now we'd better begin at the back. John, the giant sunflower seeds must be planted one by one, please, in holes that you can make with this tool called a dibber.'

John took the pointed piece of wood called a dibber, and dibbed holes at the back of the bed. He dropped a sunflower seed into each one and covered them up. They were large, long, flattish seeds. Then Mary was told to plant the nasturtium seeds so that they could climb up the trellis. She had to plant those one by one too, for they were large and rounded.

John was sent to write wooden labels for all the seeds whilst some more were being planted. He came out with a pencil and sat down on Miss Brown's barrow to write the wooden labels.

Then Peter was told to plant the Shirley poppies and the clarkia in one long row. Miss Brown showed him how to make a shallow drill or furrow with a stick. Then he shook the seeds very carefully out of the packet of poppies, and then out of the clarkia packet.

'If the wind happens to blow, just wait a minute,' said Miss Brown. 'We don't want our seeds blown all over the garden.'

Susan planted the cornflowers, and then the others planted the rest of the seeds – virginian stock all along the front edge, and candytuft, marigolds and mignonette separately behind. John produced the labels, and each row or patch was labelled correctly.

Then Miss Brown went to her little vegetable bed, and the children helped her to plant the lettuce seeds, the radishes and the mustard. She said she would plant the mustard two days later because it took a shorter time to grow than the cress.

'We will plant the cress in the shape of an S for

Susan,' she said. 'It will be fun to see it growing into a green letter!'

'Susan sowed the virginian stock very thickly,' said John. 'You told us not to shake the seeds out thickly, Miss Brown.'

'I know,' said Miss Brown. 'If people cannot sow seeds thinly it is best to mix fine sand with the seeds and sow them mixed with the sand. But virginian stock likes to be sown thickly, and it will make a lovely thick edging. We shall not thin its seedlings out at all.'

'What is thinning out?' asked Peter.

'Well,' said Miss Brown, 'you will find that although you have sown your seeds as thinly as you could, the seedlings will come up too thickly, too close together – so we shall have to pull up a good many of them, because it is much better to have a few beautifully grown, strong plants, than many poor weak ones. There will be plenty to do in our garden, Peter! We must water it if it gets dry. We must weed it – and we must thin out the seedlings.'

The children were most impatient to see their seeds grow, but it was not until two weeks had gone by that they saw the first hint of green in their flower-bed. The candytuft and virginian stock pushed up first and the others followed quickly. The giant sunflowers and nasturtiums were last, but they grew very fast once they were up, and it was not long before the first nasturtium began to climb up the trellis.

The garden was the greatest fun! The children watered it when they came to school. They weeded it when it wanted weeding. They thinned out the thick seedlings carefully and watched the rest grow into sturdy and beautiful plants.

Miss Brown's mustard and cress grew well, and the first time it was ready to cut, Miss Brown asked the children to sea and gave them good thick sandwiches of the delicious green-stuff. The lettuces grew too, and would soon be ready for salad, and the radishes grew large and red. The children tasted these and loved them, though Susan said hers had burnt a hole in her tongue, it was so hot!

The peas and beans they had grown came into flower and smelt very sweet.

And oh, what a joy it was when the flowers blossomed! The virginian stock was a mass of pink, white and yellow. The poppies danced in all colours. The nasturtiums gave brilliant flowers for the classroom. The candytuft held up heads of red and pink and white, and the clarkia grew rosettes of red and pink and lasted for weeks in the schoolroom vases.

The marigolds bloomed on and on and on, and the cornflowers were made into a bunch for Miss Brown's bedroom. The classroom smelt of mignonette every day when that quaint red-brown flower bloomed, and everyone loved it.

'Its name is French for "little darling" and it's a jolly good name!' said Mary, sniffing its fragrance.

'The giant sunflowers will be out soon,' said John. 'Miss Brown, one looks right over the wall! Their faces are simply enormous – as big as my dinner-plate!'

'They will give us many seeds for the finches and sparrows!' said Miss Brown. 'We will save them and dry them when the flowers are over.'

'What fun we've had with our garden!' said Susan. 'I'd like to begin it all over again, Miss Brown.'

'Well, so you shall!' said Miss Brown, with a laugh. 'Every year you can begin again – that's what gardeners love, Susan!'

May. Having Fun with the Birds.

THE FOUR children at Miss Brown's school all loved the birds. They loved hearing them practising their spring songs in February and March, they enjoyed wathing for the first swallows and house-martins in April, and they were most excited when they knew where a nest was.

'Miss Brown, couldn't we hang up a nesting-box somewhere?' asked John. 'The garden is full of tits, and I am sure they would nest here if they had a proper box.'

'Well, we'll buy one,' said Miss Brown. 'They are quite cheap.'

'I've just had two shillings from one of my uncles,' said John. 'Would that buy a nesting-box?'

'Oh yes!' said Miss Brown. 'You shall go with me to buy it after tea, John.'

So John went proudly with Miss Brown to buy the nesting-box. It had a little hole near the top for the tits to go in and out, and the over-hanging lid could be lifted up and down so that John might see if any birds had begun to build later on.

'Where shall we put it?' said John next morning.

'Let's go into the garden and see,' said Miss Brown. So she and the children trooped out and had a good look around. There was a spruce fir-tree not too far from the schoolroom window and Miss Brown stopped underneath it.

'This tree will do well,' she said. 'Now we will put the box under this bough here, close to the trunk – and we will make it face north-east, as driving rain seldom comes from that direction. Where's that big nail, John? Hammer it in.'

John hammered in the nail, and Miss Brown hung up the box. It was brown, and matched the colour of the tree-trunk. John lifted up the lid and peeped in.

'Nothing at all inside,' he said. 'Won't it be exciting when I lift up the lid and see a nest beginning to be made!'

'It will,' said Miss Brown, 'but you will have to remember that if you do too much peeping *then*, John, the birds may desert the nest.'

'Miss Brown, Miss Brown, when will the birds come and look at the box to see if it is a good nesting-place!' cried Susan.

'Oh, to-day, I hope,' said Miss Brown.

'Can't we let them know we've put a fine nesting-box here for them?' wondered Peter. 'Miss Brown! Why couldn't we hang a nice bone under the nesting box? Then the tits would be sure to find that and would look inside the box too.

'That's a very good idea, Peter,' said Miss Brown. She sent Peter for a bone and he hung it under the box. Then they all trooped indoors to lessons.

'I wish I could have a nesting-box too,' sighed Peter. 'But I haven't any money. I suppose if I tried to make a nest and put it in a tree, it wouldn't be much good, would it, Miss Brown?'

'I'm afraid not,' said Miss Brown. 'But I will tell you what you can do, if you like, Peter – you can bring an old tin, or an old kettle to school and we will put it under the hedge at the bottom of the school garden.

There are two robins hunting about there for a nesting-place – maybe they will choose your kettle! They love to build in something like that, you know.'

'Oh, good!' said Peter – and when he arrived at school that afternoon he brought with him two tins, an old saucepan and a kettle too!'

Everybody laughed. 'I'm surprised you didn't bring a coal-scuttle and a dustbin as well!' said John.

'Well, I thought I'd give the birds a good choice of nesting-places,' said Peter happily. 'May I choose my hiding-places for them at playtime, Miss Brown?'

'Of course,' said Miss Brown. So at eleven o'clock the four children ran to look for good places to put the tins. Peter put one half-way up a hedge. He put the saucepan in a ditch. He put the other tin on a bank, and the kettle he threw among some nettles.

'There!' he said. 'Robins! Choose which you like to nest in – and mind you do choose one, or I shall be most disappointed.'

The two girls felt a little left out of all this, and they wondered how they could have fun with the birds too.

'What can *I* do?' said Mary.

'I will tell you something nice to do,' said Miss Brown. 'Yesterday as I went along the lane I saw a post where cows rub themselves and sometimes leave their hairs. And, goodness me, how the birds were quarrelling about those hairs! Then a little farther on I came to Farmer Straws' hen-yard, and there were about twenty sparrows there squabbling over the few feathers that the hens had let fall. And . . .'

'But, Miss Brown, what did they want the hairs and the feathers for?' interrupted Susan.

'They wanted them for a nest-lining,' said Miss Brown. 'And whilst it is easy to find moss, roots, fibres, dead leaves and so on, to make the nests themselves, it is quite difficult to find the softer material for a lining – hair, wool, feathers and fluff.'

'What was the something nice you said I could do, then?' asked Mary. 'Find some nest-linings?'

'Yes,' said Miss Brown. 'I have an old net bag here in my desk. Look!' Miss Brown pulled it out. 'Well, would you like to collect all the soft things you can, Mary, and fill the bag with them? It will be a lucky-bag for the birds then and they can come and pull out whatever they want.'

'Oh, I'd simply love to do that!' cried Mary, pleased. 'I shall collect all the feathers I can – and ask Mummy for the fluff out of the carpet-sweeper each day – and get the wool off the hedges, where the sheep have scraped against it – and I can get the hairs out of my hair-brush!'

'And I'll give you mine too!' cried Susan.

'And my mother has been making a rug, and she has got lots of little bits of wool over!' said Peter. 'You shall have those, Mary. Oh, your lucky-bag will soon be full!'

Mary took the net bag home and crammed it full of all the soft things she could think of – hairs from everyone's brushes, strands of wool from her work-basket, feathers from the hen-run, wool from the brambles, fluff from the carpet-sweeper, snippings from the rag-bag, and even hairs brushed out of her dog's coat.

The others brought things too and soon the bag was full of soft bits and was ready to put up. Miss Brown tied it flat to a branch of a tree near the window, and then the children kept an eye on it.

'Good gracious!' said Peter, in the middle of the next lesson, 'there are seven birds on Mary's lucky-bag already, Miss Brown. Do look!'

Everyone looked. There were three sparrows, a robin, two chaffinches and a hedge-sparrow all pulling busily at the contents of the bag. The sparrows flew off with feathers. The robin took a mouthful of hairs. The chaffinches took the fluff from the sweeper and the hedge-sparrow took a beakful of everything!

'Oh, isn't it a success!' said Mary, pleased. 'Oh, Miss Brown, isn't it funny to think that some of the nests round about are lined with my hairs! I like to think of that.'

'Miss Brown!' There's a tit gone right into my nesting-box!' cried John suddenly. 'I saw it. Oh, do you think it is going to nest there?'

'We'll see,' said Miss Brown. Then she suddenly saw that seven-year-old Susan was looking very red, as if she were going to cry. 'Whatever's the matter, Susan?' she asked.

'Everybody's done something for the birds except me,' said Susan, a tear rolling down her cheek.

'Oh, don't be silly, dear,' said Miss Brown. 'You are sharing everything with the others.'

'It isn't the same as having something all to myself,' said Susan. 'John's got his nesting-box. Peter's got his tins and things. Mary's got her lucky-bag. I've got nothing.'

'Well, you shall give the birds their bath,' said Miss Brown. 'I was thinking that now the hot weather is coming we must put out a bath for them. Have you anything at home that would do for a bath?'

'Miss Brown, Susan's mother has had a new sink put into her scullery!' cried John. 'Couldn't Susan have the old sink for a bird-bath? We could dig a hole for it in the ground and put it there so that it looked like a little pond!'

Everyone was most excited about this, and after tea that day Susan's father wheeled the old sink to school, and dug a hole for it in the middle of the lawn. It just fitted the tink. Then Susan's father dug out a little narrow bed round the sink, and gave Susan a shilling to go and buy some double daisy plants to put round the sink.

'It looks exactly like a pond with flowers growing round it!' cried Susan, as she and Miss Brown planted the pink and white button daisies. 'Oh, I'm so happy, Miss Brown. I think I've got the nicest thing of all to do for the birds.'

'Well, you must keep your pond nicely filled with water,' said Miss Brown. 'Not too deep, or you won't get the smaller birds bathing in it.'

And now all the children were pleased because they were each having fun with the birds in their own way. A pair of tits were already nesting in John's box, and he lifted up the lid very gently to see how the nest was getting on. The box was soon half-full of nesting-material, mostly moss, and hairs taken from the lucky-bag.

One of the greatest excitements was on the day that Peter went to examine his tins for the sixth time to see if any robin was nesting – and he found the kettle half-full of dead leaves and moss. He spied a robin nearby with a leaf in its mouth and he rushed off to Miss Brown in delight.

'They've chosen the kettle, they've chosen the kettle!' he shouted. 'The robins are beginning to build.'

'Well, that's lovely,' said Miss Brown. 'We have tits building in John's nesting-box, robins building in your old kettle, all the birds of the garden pulling treasures from Mary's lucky-bag, and any amount of them splashing in Susan's bird-bath all day long!'

'Yes – it's lovely,' said Susan happily. She was so proud of her bird-pond. The double daisies had grown well around it, and the birds looked sweet, splashing away in the water, sending drops all over the daisies. The robin loved a bath and was always splashing there. The thrushes and blackbirds came every morning and evening. The chaffinches came when the bath was empty, and the sparrows hopped in and out all day long. It was the greatest fun to watch.

And there was more fun to come too, for both robin and tit laid eggs, and hatched them into tiny birds. How proud Peter and John were when they saw their young families hopping about the garden, learning to look after themselves!

'This is another thing we'll do every year!' said Mary. 'We'll always have fun with the birds in the spring-time!'

THE NAUGHTIEST GIRL QUIZ

If you've read all four of Enid Blyton's original stories about the Naughtiest Girl, then you will have no problem with this quiz by Tony Summerfield . . .

1. The uniform of Whyteleafe School is in which colours?
a) brown and orange
b) blue and silver
c) blue and yellow

2. Which Boy looks after the gardens at Whyteleafe?
a) Martin Follett
b) John Terry
c) Julian Holland

3. What is the name of Elizabeth Allen's governess?
a) Miss Scott
b) Miss Thomas
c) Miss White

4. Who is the first form teacher in the Naughtiest Girl?
a) Miss Ranger
b) Miss Stevens
c) Miss Timms

5. In *The Naughtiest Girl is a Monitor*, who organises a midnight feast, but doesn't invite Elizabeth?
a) Arabella Buckley
b) Belinda Green
c) Helen Marsden

6. In the Naughtiest Girl books, what is the name of the music master who takes Elizabeth for piano lessons?
a) Mr Johns
b) Mr Lewis
c) Mr Warlow

7. In *The Naughtiest Girl is a Monitor*, what is the name of the Allen's cook?
a) Mrs Jenks
b) Mrs Marks
c) Mrs Tonks

8. In *The Naughtiest Girl Again*, who is reprimanded at the meeting for not feeding her guinea pigs?
a) Dora
b) Doris
c) Dorothy

ANSWERS

1. a); 2. b); 3. a); 4. a); 5. a); 6. b); 7. a); 8. b)

THE NAUGHTIEST GIRL
THROUGH THE YEARS . . .

1940

1962

1967

1971

1973

1979

1986

1999

2007